Diary of an Accidental Witch

SCHOOL TRIP

TO THE READERS WHO HAVE SENT US LETTERS AND DRAWINGS, THANK YOU! WE THINK YOU ARE MAGICAL, AND THIS BOOK IS ESPECIALLY FOR YOU, H. AND P. XX

TO MY LONG-SUFFERING SISTER SARAH (MRS. COTTA) AND THE LOVELY CHILDREN AT IWADE SCHOOL, WHO SHE READS THESE MAGICAL BOOKS TO - K.S.

tiger tales

5 River Road, Suite 128, Wilton, CT 06897
Published in the United States 2024
Originally published in Great Britain 2022
by Little Tiger Press Limited
Text copyright © 2022 Perdita & Honor Cargill
Illustrations copyright © 2022 Katie Saunders
ISBN-13: 978-1-6643-4078-7
ISBN-10: 1-6643-4078-5
Printed in China
STP/3800/0546/0324
All rights reserved
2 4 6 8 10 9 7 5 3 1

www.tigertalesbooks.com

Diary of an Accidental Witch

SCHOOL TRIP

BY PERDITA & HONOR CARGILL
ILLUSTRATED BY KATIE SAUNDERS

tiger tales

V. V. EXTREEEMELY PRIVATE

PROPERTY OF BEA BLACK

*1 Piggoty Lane,
Little Spellshire,
Spellshire*

WARNING: Serious risk of being turned into a ~~toad~~ NEWT if you read this diary....

ABOUT ME!

- **Name:** Bea Black
- **Age:** 11 and a half ↗ *BEST place to live in the WHOLE WORLD*
- **Lives:** No. 1 Piggoty Lane, Little Spellshire
- **Lives with:** My dad, Ben (v. good at being a weather scientist. V. BAD at cooking)
- **Goes to school at:** Little Spellshire's School of Extraordinary Arts
- **Best friends:** Ash Namdar (NOT a witch) and Amara Chukwu, Puck Berry, Winnie Ross, and Fabi Lightening (all very witchy). Also, Stan (froggy and magical in his own way).
- **Favorite food:** Anything from Taffy Tallywick's teashop. Also, fluffmallows, troll's toenails, and skullsquigglers.

SATURDAY, JANUARY 1

10:00 a.m. Home

NEW YEAR'S RESOLUTIONS

- Get better at all things WITCHY, including things I'm already quite good at, like taking care of frogs and flying and basic levitation AND all the things I'm ~~a bit~~ VERY useless at like potions.
- Master all the **GO** tactics (ask Blair to show me how to do the loop-the-loop properly).
- Learn all about witchy history and TRADITIONS so all the other witches don't think I'm a TOADBRAIN.
- Persuade Dad that we NEED a family dog.

EVEN HARDER NEW YEAR'S RESOLUTIONS

- Stop feeling like the NEW GIRL all the time
- ~~Make friends with~~ Get along better with Hunter and Izzy and especially Blair Smith-Smythe!
- Become the kind of CONFIDENT and GROWN-UP witch who isn't worried about ~~anything~~ everything—especially not about my very first away-from-home *WITCHY* SCHOOL TRIP!
- Don't tell anyone non-witchy ↗ELSE about the WITCH THING....

10:27 a.m.

Okay, okay, so I *did* tell Ash about the witchy thing because once he'd seen me levitating a frog and then found a large, magical Finkelspark EGG under my bed, I really didn't have much choice. Anyway, I can't help being glad that he knows—now I can hang out with my best non-witch friend and my best witch schoolfriends at the same time (which is a huge relief because keeping them apart was very, very, VERY stressful).

10:35 a.m.

Stan is hopping up and down in front of me like he's got ants in his pants.* I think he's trying to remind me that I have a best friend FROG to share secrets with. It's true—I can tell Stan *everything*. He wouldn't tell anyone ... even if he could talk.

10:41 a.m.

Wait ... I suppose he could tell the other class frogs about all my DISASTERS?

*If frogs wore pants.

Except no ... I can't imagine it. My secrets *are* safe with Stan. It was very nice of Mr. Muddy to let me take him home for the holidays because, strictly speaking, class frogs are meant to stay in school.

"I might as well give you permission," he'd said with a grin. "*Unofficially*, I'm well aware that frog's been practically living at your house for weeks!"

Stan and I are inseparable, and although it's not always easy to tell, I like to think he's as happy about that as I am.

7:55 p.m.

Me and Dad just got home from having dinner at Ash's house. Iranian New Year isn't for a while, but Mrs. Namdar had still prepared a feast of chicken and crusty golden rice and love cake. Given how ~~terrible~~ inventive Dad is at cooking, it's very lucky that we live next door to the Namdars.

Mr. Namdar—who's an engineer in the army and away a lot—was home for the vacation. He looks like Ash and is very smiley. He is also very ~~inkwizzi~~ inquisitive. First, he wanted to know how we were settling in in Little Spellshire and I said I could never imagine living anywhere else, and Dad said it was very nice, but that he was having a hard time writing his book.

"It's called *Understanding Little Spellshire's Most Peculiar Microclimate*," he said.

"Good luck understanding *that*," replied Mr. Namdar

at the exact moment an unexpected lightning bolt struck the windowpane and everyone laughed (except Dad). Then Mr. Namdar started INTERROGATING me about school.

"But what kind of 'arts' do you learn at a School of Extraordinary Arts?" he kept asking. "Is it mostly drawing and painting?"

I thought back to last semester and making enchanted Winter Solstice masks with Mr. Zicasso.

"Um ... there is a lot of painting," I said.

"Dancing?"

I had a flashback of doing a witchy conga at the Halloween Ball and nodded. "Yes, we do a lot of dancing."

"What about drama?"

"Definitely!"

Maybe we didn't do the kind of acting lessons Mr. Namdar was imagining, but there was always A LOT of drama at Extraordinary!

SUNDAY, JANUARY 2

6:33 p.m. Home

Spent the day cloud-spotting with Dad. He loves clouds even more than he loves frogs or thundersnow and almost as much as he loves me. All the snow had melted and it was warm, so we lay on our backs and he pointed out a nimbostratus and a stratocumulus. I pointed out a cloud shaped like a dragon and one shaped like a toad. Stan didn't point out anything, but he seemed to have a good time.

And now we're going to order pizza because Dad forgot to buy any food for dinner.

9:01 p.m.

Perfect Little Spellshire day.

MONDAY, JANUARY 3

11:01 a.m. Home

Can't believe it's the last day of vacation and now I need to stop lazing around, eating fizzy skullsquigglers (although that is a Very Nice Thing to do), and wash and iron my school uniform. Ms. Sparks always says, "Extraordinary witches must learn how to do everyday, useful, Ordinary skills," and Ms. Sparks is the kind of principal who is usually right.*

2:33 p.m.

Oooops, my school pinafore is now very short and there's a singe hole in the back of my cape. It looks like I've inherited Dad's washing and ironing skills.

*Also, I don't know how to do any washing and ironing spells yet.

3:45 p.m. Winnie's house

Went over to Winnie's so she could help me with some of my vacation homework that I hadn't ~~started~~ finished. Amara and Puck and Fabi were already there, and everyone was talking about going back to school.

"It's going to be the best semester yet," says Puck. "I CAN'T WAIT!"

Odd. He's not usually *that* enthusiastic about school.

"Me, neither," says Winnie with a big smile. "Multiplication tables!" She gives a dreamy sigh.

"Um … I was talking about the school trip," says Puck, looking at her like she's a (friendly) alien.

Of course! We've been talking about it all vacation—only two weeks to go. We don't know *where* we're going, but we're very excited and a little bit nervous.*

8:55 p.m. Home

Winnie said the teachers would probably tell us EVERYTHING about the trip tomorrow. I'll probably stop worrying when I know where we're going.

*Especially ME!

TUESDAY, JANUARY 4

9:02 a.m. School

The first thing Mr. Muddy said when he saw me and Stan was that I could stay as frog monitor, but I was only halfway through saying thank you when Hunter started yelling, "SIR, SIR, TELL US ABOUT THE SCHOOL TRIP!"

"Please tell us, Mr. Muddy!" we all begged.

"I know! I know!" Li Lightening was practically self-levitating with excitement. "Is it Ogre's Causeway?"

Mr. Muddy shook his head.

"Foggy Bottom?" suggested Polly Bucket.

"Goblins' Grotto?"

"Dragon's Crag?"

"STOP!" Mr. Muddy held up his hands to ward off our questions. "You are a terrible class for all talking at the same time!"

"*BUT, SIR, WHERE—*"

"Be patient, little witches. You'll be told as soon as the decision has been made."

"Wait, what?" Blair did not look impressed. "You mean *nobody* knows where we're going?"

"Not yet. It's a very tricky decision and not to be rushed. As Ms. Sparks always says: 'The trip must be right for the witches and the witches must be right for the trip!' So for now—" he grinned, flicked his wand, and schedules started raining down on to our desks— "let's concentrate on double physics. Such fun!"

Schedule: Sixth Grade (Homeroom Teacher: Mr. Muddy): Spring Semester
Student Name: BEA BLACK

Time	Monday	Tuesday	Wednesday	Thursday	Friday
09:00–09:15	Homeroom	Homeroom	Homeroom	Homeroom	Homeroom
09:20–10:00	Chem/Biology	Physics	Geography	Physics	Chem/Biology
10:05–10:50	Chem/Biology	Physics	Geography	Physics	Chem/Biology
10:55–11:15	Break	Break	Break	Break	Break
11:20–12:00	Math	Math	Math	English	English
12:05–1:05	Lunch	Lunch	Lunch	Lunch	Lunch
1:10–1:55	PD	PD	Whole School Assembly	PD	PD
2:00–2:45	History	PE	Chem/Biology	Zoology	Friday Lecture
2:50–3:30	Art	PE	Chem/Biology	History	Geography

11:01 a.m.

Breaktime and we're all eating fluffmallows and placing bets as to where we're going on our trip. I've never heard of most of the places.

"What's Goblins' Grotto?" I ask.

Blair rolls her eyes. "It's a grotto with goblins, duh."

Right. "What's Foggy Bottom then?"

"It's a *foggy*—"

"Never mind that," interrupts Winnie, waving the new schedule in our faces. "We've got our first *geography* class tomorrow!"

I thought only Winnie would be more excited about geography than Foggy Bottom, but everyone stops talking about the trip and starts discussing the new teacher, Dr. Pellicano.

"Has anyone met her yet?" asks Amara.

None of us has even *seen* her.

"Maybe she's not here yet," suggests Fabi. "My dad told me he'd heard she was on an expedition to the lair of the Abominable Snowman."

"The Abominable Snowman?" I giggle. "That's not a real thing."

And now everyone's laughing at me. *SIGH*.

11:13 a.m.

Okay, so now I know that not only is the Abominable Snowman real, but he comes from a long line of VERY SHY Abominable Snowmen and has a wife and three mini-Abominables. According to Hunter, only a *toadbrain* wouldn't have known that. So I probably shouldn't have admitted that all I knew about Dr. Pellicano was her name (because I read it in the school newsletter).

"But she's FAMOUS." Izzi is shocked.

"Classic Bea," says Blair, waggling her eyebrows at her friends. "She knows less about the witch world than my two-year-old sister."

I turn red. That might be true, but there's no need for her to point it out. Classic *Blair* (looks like I'm not going to get along much better with her this semester than last). But even my best friends seem a little shocked that I don't know about Dr. Pellicano.

"But she's flown across the whole wide world," says Amara in awe.

"Lots* of people have done that!" I point out.

"Not on a broomstick," says Blair with a snort.

11:25 a.m.

It looks like Mr. Smith has spent the vacation coming up with more inventive ways to TORTURE us in math. But I can tell he's missed us. I know we're his favorite class, even if some of us** can't remember what the difference is between a ~~parra~~ parallelogram and a ~~rom~~ rhombus (much less spell them).

*Well, a few.
**ME.

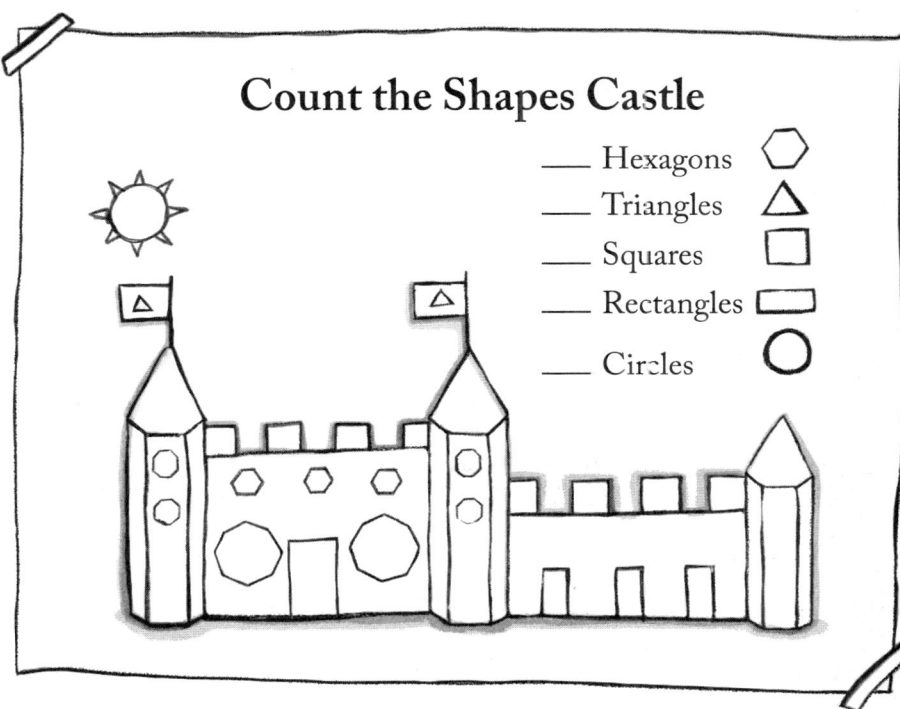

12:00 p.m.

Oh, dear. Mr. Smith said we were the worst class he'd EVER taught and (in his words) "wouldn't know how to work together to solve a simple math problem if our lives depended on it." I think he was ~~eggsa~~ exaggerating.

All this math has made me hungry for lunch. I wonder if I'm witchy enough now to have developed a taste for witch sausages?

12:33 p.m.
EEEEEEUGH.

NO! WITCH SAUSAGES ARE STILL DISGUSTING.

1:55 p.m.

There's a message for us on the bulletin board:

> Dear Year Sevens,
>
> Please stop asking questions about the school trip.
>
> While curiosity is to be encouraged in witches (although not in cats), PESTERING teachers is to be discouraged.
>
> You'll be told what you need to know by the time you need to know it.

3:16 p.m.

First **GO** match of the semester and we won!

We WON! *WE WON!*

Final score:

| DODOS: 17 | DRAGONS: 15 |

I scored SIX goals and pulled off a Stealthy Slither without falling off my broomstick, which surprised Hunter so much that *he* fell off and got stuck in a bush.

"FOUL!" he shouted at the exact same time as Ms. Celery boomed: "Good work, Bea!"

I never thought I'd say this, but Ms. Celery is turning out to be one of my favorite teachers.

6:03 p.m. Home

"How was your first day back, Bec?" asks Dad, rushing into the kitchen like a tornado's chasing him.* *Dragons!* He has no idea how hard it is when he asks questions like this. There's so much I want to tell him and I *can't*.

6:28 p.m.

Our conversation went something like this:

---

*To be fair, it is VERY windy.

ME (aloud): Fine.

(inside head): *WILD! You have no idea!*

DAD: But what did you learn?

ME (aloud): Oh, nothing much really ... some useful geometry, a few experiments about moving forces in physics, and some new tactics in PE. Oh, and NOTHING about the school trip.

(inside head): *So much! Some useful geometry, how to levitate Fabi to the ceiling and back down again without dropping him, AND I played* **GO**, *which is the best broomstick-flying sport in the universe. I scored seven goals, but only six of them went down the Great Chimney so one counted as a foul, but I pulled off a Boggle Dodge and next week Ms. Celery is going to teach us the Skeleshaker. Oh, and Hunter fell off his broomstick into a bush! Oh, and NOTHING about the school trip.*

6:41 p.m.

Now that I think about it, I *do* have something I can tell Dad. "I don't feel like the NEW GIRL anymore," I announce proudly.

It's true! I might know as much about Abominable Snowmen and other witch-world stuff as your average gerbil* and I might be more worried about the school trip than the others AND, of course, I can't do as much magic as the others can, but I AM catching up! It's not like I could have levitated Fabi on my first day. I know where to go (usually) and I know (almost) everyone's names and I LOVE all the frogs *and* I'm used to the spiders and the mayhem.

I belong at Extraordinary!

---

*Or Blair's two-year-old sister!

WEDNESDAY, JANUARY 5

8:55 a.m. School

Except for one rainy afternoon counting cars on Main Street when we were in third grade, we didn't do geography at my last school. I am SO excited about witch geography!

11:01 a.m.

NOT excited about witch geography anymore....

DR. PELLICANO IS TERRIFYING.

"Stop chattering!" was the first thing she said, literally appearing without warning in a puff of smoke. "You're worse than a colony of blue-footed boobies, *kaaak-kaak-kaaak*. Much worse! At least the booby finds better things to talk about than fluffmallows and fashion."

Eeeek! How long had she been listening to us? We looked at each other nervously.

Dr. Pellicano didn't seem like a witch-world-famous adventurer. She was like an upside-down exclamation mark. She was very tall and very skinny and dressed all in black, with jet-black hair in a perfect round bun on the top of her head.

"*Dribbling dragons*," muttered Amara under her breath. "She's strict."

"Pay attention!" barked the new teacher. "Which of you can tell me where blue-footed boobies live?"

Winnie was the only one brave enough to put up her hand. "Um ... at the seaside?"

"I was hoping for something more specific."

With a mighty TUT, Dr. Pellicano flicked her wand, and a map of South America appeared on the wall behind her.

"Fascinating place, the Galápagos," she said, jabbing at a cluster of little islands. "Wolf Volcano! Kicker Rock! The Santa Cruz lava tunnels! Ah, the adventures I had. Sadly, *our* geographical adventures will have to take place closer to home."

The map of the Galápagos disappeared, to be replaced by one of North America.

"We shall begin with your immediate landscape—" one spot on the map began to glow, Little Spellshire!—"and I shall teach you how to find your way around it because there's nothing more annoying than a witch merrily flying about in the sky without a clue about the ground that lies beneath. Witches must respect the Earth as well as the skies ... and that respect starts with remembering to pick up our litter."

She shot a terrible glare at Hunter, who froze (LITERALLY*) in the act of dropping an empty fluffmallow packet into Winnie's schoolbag.

I bet the Abominable Snowman was scared of Dr. Pellicano.

---

*He didn't "defrost" until the end of class!

> *Homework: Pick up every piece of litter on your way home and properly dispose of it by Earth-loving means. Repeat every day for the rest of your life.*

1:10 p.m.

First assembly of the semester in the Great Hall, and it's the usual crush and scuffle in the sixth-grade row to make sure that we're sitting next to our friends.

"Welcome back to Extraordinary!" Ms. Sparks is on her feet. "I hope you all had a wonderful vacation and have come back full of magic beans, ready for all the hard work and fun that lies ahead. Whatever challenges this semester has in store for you—be it mastering advanced transformations—" she looks over sympathetically at the tenth graders—"or battling broomsticks on the **GO** pitch—" Ms. Celery leaps to her feet and punches the air— "or even—" now Ms. Sparks is looking at us—"setting off on your first Extraordinary school trip, I know you will all do your very best for yourselves AND for each other. Remember that many witch hats are *often better than one!"*

There's a little round of applause for this from the other teachers.

"Now, speaking of school trips, I'm sure the sixth graders are anxious to know where they're going."

Anxious? The suspense is KILLING us.

"Well...." Ms. Sparks pauses and looks at our row very carefully. "There's one place that keeps coming to mind—"

BANG!

1:15 p.m.

It was Mrs. Slater, the school receptionist, crashing in through the doors on her broom and sending several witches flying.* Now she's up on the stage, muttering in Ms. Sparks's ear, and even from here I can tell it's *angry* muttering....

"*I see....*" Ms. Sparks sighs a disappointed sigh, and a tiny halo of sparks starts to dance around her head (never a good sign). "Do any of you have anything you'd like to share with the rest of us?"

*She's a REALLY BAD FLIER!!

She looks around the hall with the kind of teacher look that makes me feel guilty even when I haven't done anything wrong.

Wait, *have* I done something wrong? Everyone's looking at everyone else—this is **VERY STRESSFUL.**

Ms. Sparks lets us suffer for a minute and then says, "The witch responsible for filling the mini-witch toilets with enchanted OCTOPUSES has precisely **TEN SECONDS** to own up before I turn him into a squid. Ten, nine, eight, *seven*...."

Very slowly, Puck raises his hand.

1:55 p.m.

Sadly, that was the last we heard about the school trip. Ms. Sparks spent the rest of assembly lecturing us on why it is rarely a good idea to do magic in toilets. Apparently, octopuses—even enchanted ones that pop like bubbles and disappear after a few hours—can be a nasty surprise when found in the bottom of the bowl.

2:05 p.m.

Miss Lupo says we're going to study basic healing potions this semester. That's good news as I'm quite an accident-prone witch.

"Proper mastery of healing requires a combination of sound potion skills *and* relevant word spells, so Madam Binx and I will be coordinating our lessons," she announces. "And I advise you all to *pay attention* as you never know when you—or someone else—might need a little 'repair.' You can't always assume there'll be a grown-up around to help you—especially when you're away from home—"

"Please, Miss Lupo, do *you* know where we're going on the trip?" shout out five witches at once.

"I know where *I'd* like to send you," says Miss Lupo, swishing her wand and breaking up a tug-of-war between Raven and Izzi over the last fluffy quill. "*Pocus-focus*, witches—one of the most common ingredients in healing potions is the spiderweb. Take notes, please." She turns to the board behind her and writes:

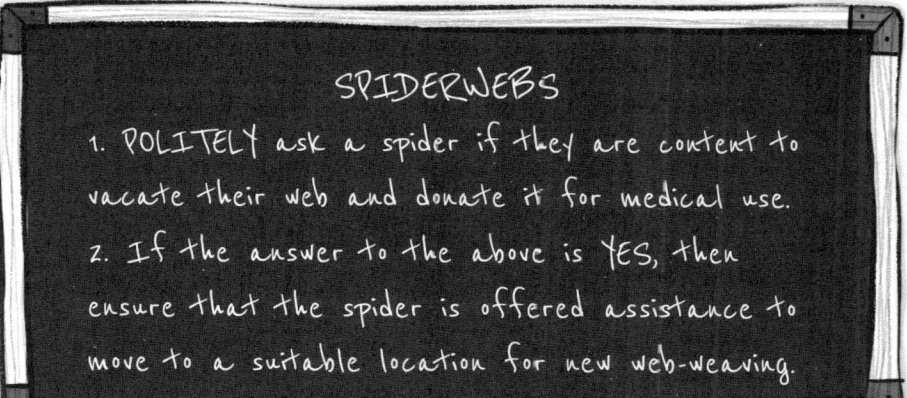

SPIDERWEBS

1. POLITELY ask a spider if they are content to vacate their web and donate it for medical use.
2. If the answer to the above is YES, then ensure that the spider is offered assistance to move to a suitable location for new web-weaving.

She flicks her wand at a drawer behind her and says, "Here are some I collected earlier."

The drawer shoots open and c *shiver* of spiderwebs float out, and one by one they drop onto our desks.

"Lucky me," whispers Blair, wiggling her eyebrows at me. "Mine's still got a spider in it. What *shall* I do with it?"

2:09 p.m.

I ducked just in time.

5:25 p.m.

Me and Winnie and Amara and Fabi are staying late

to help Puck clean the mini-witch toilets. Annoyed that nobody else from our class is helping because it's a VERY big mess and we're not allowed to use magic.

6:45 p.m. Home

Dad says the weather in the Galápagos is very interesting and he wishes he were writing about that instead. "Maybe that'll be my next book," he says, "when I've finished with Little Spellshire."

9:13 p.m.

Must remember to ask Puck to show me how to do that spell. SO COOL!

THURSDAY, JANUARY 6

11:25 a.m. School

"Webs and words!" Madam Binx beams. "Two of my favorite things! Let's make this healing charm nice and strong with a good rhyme. *Mmmmm*, what goes with spider?"

11:35 a.m.

Nothing rhymes with spider. Or web.
    My brain hurts.

2:35 p.m.

Learning about the difference between wolf and wolfwish sounds in zoology, and Puck and Hunter are arguing over which of them is better at howling.

Professor Agu says that if we could communicate half as well as wolfy animals do then he'd be very impressed.

2:40 p.m.

Howling is fun, but Professor Agu has just given the whole class a detention for being "wild and disorderly."

3:55 p.m.

If they don't tell us soon where we're going on our school trip, we will all EXPLODE with ~~nerves~~ impatience and it will take more than spiderwebs to put us back together.

FRIDAY, JANUARY 7

9:23 a.m. School

"Let's start today with a fun little challenge," says Miss Lupo, disappearing inside a big cupboard in the corner of the room labeled *Very Peculiar Teaching Aids for the Modern Witch*.

"Found it!" She emerges with a *ta-da* and drops a *very realistic-looking* model of a *hand* on the table in the middle of the room.

"EEEEEEEEUGH!" say Amara and Winnie and me.

"YUCK!" say Raven and Li and Izzi.

"What are we supposed to do with that?" asks Puck.

Fabi is peering at it very closely. "There's a cut

on its finger."

"Is that real blood, Miss Lupo?" Hunter asks.

"Don't be ridiculous," says Miss Lupo briskly. "It's *teaching* blood, and what you're going to do with Hand—" she looked at the thing fondly—"is *heal* it."

"But we don't know how to do that," Izzi protests.

"Then put your heads together and figure it out. I'm sure you'll get there in the end if you work together nicely." (Miss Lupo doesn't *sound* sure.) "There's a box of fresh spiderwebs on the shelf. I'll be back in twenty minutes to see how it's going. Good luck."

And then she just *leaves*!

10:15 a.m.

I don't think we did very well on the "fun little challenge"....

We all stared at Hand for a few minutes and then Blair decided to take charge. "*I* know how to do it. Everyone needs to stand back." She cleared her throat. "Webs of spiders, shells of snails, blood of bats and legs of logs—"

"Um," Winnie cut in, "it would be legs of *frogs*. Obviously. Except that we're only supposed to be using *webs*."

"You can't PROVE logs don't have legs." Blair wasn't backing down.

"But it's *cruel* to use bats' blood." Polly was almost in tears.

"It's worse to use frogs' legs!" I said, covering Stan's little ears.

And just like that, the class was in an uproar! Hunter was arguing with Li, and Raven was arguing with Fabi, and Blair was still arguing with Winnie. A large family of snails was trying to evacuate the classroom as quickly as possible,* Puck was hanging upside down from the ceiling pretending to be a sloth, and Izzi had knocked over a cauldron full of something green and slimy. It was CHAOS!!!

"WAIT!" I shouted so loudly that everyone

*NOT very quickly.

stopped arguing and turned to stare at me. "Where's Hand??"

"It's on the—" Blair stopped. Hand was definitely NOT on the table anymore.

"*Aiieeeeeee!*" squealed Polly, pointing with a shaky finger at Hand, which was *waving* from a high shelf.

Izzi screamed and jumped on a desk. "It's *alive!*"

"It's not alive," Hunter said. "It's just a silly model."

At that, Hand leaped down and landed with a **SLAAAAPPPPPP** on Hunter's desk.

"AHHHHHHH—it *is* alive!!!" he screamed.

Broomsticks! Hand was clearly *very annoyed* now. It was hopping all over the room— pulling books off shelves, hurling sheets of homework out of the window, tugging braids and ponytails, and spraying "blood" EVERYWHERE!

"*Oh, dear*," said a horribly familiar voice from the doorway.

As one, we turned, looked at Ms. Sparks, and PANICKED.

"Would anyone like to explain? No? Nobody? Well, I suppose you've all had a *hand* in this particular disaster, *haha!*"

None of us was laughing—especially not Miss Lupo, who flew in through the open window, took one look at the mess in her classroom, and said in the kind of voice that would freeze a sunbeam, "I. Am. Disappointed."

"But not, I fear, *surprised*," said Ms. Sparks. She shared a long look with Miss Lupo and then nodded firmly, "Yes. That's decided then." And without telling us *what* had decided *what*, she said she had something very important to do and left.

It's a shame Miss Lupo didn't go with her. She was VERY angry.

"It doesn't look like you've done much healing, sixth grade," she said through gritted teeth. "Clearly, *some* of you weren't listening when I told you to work nicely together."

She swished her wand and in a second, Hand lay still and perfectly healed in the middle of the table.

"Count yourselves lucky that this *mayhem* happened at school and not in the WILD. Anything could have happened!"

10:55 a.m.

Spent the rest of the class doing non-magical cleaning up and having Quiet-Time-to-Think-About-Our-Behavior. *Broomsticks.*

11:46 a.m.

Madam Binx has set us a list of healing spells to learn by heart, including this one:

> Four little arms and four little legs
> That wove these webs of silken threads,
> We ask you now this cut to seal
> Until our patient is all healed!

12:12 p.m.

Ms. Sparks wants to see us after lunch. This is turning out to be a very STRESSFUL day.

1:12 p.m.

"Find somewhere to sit." Ms. Sparks ushered us into her office. "Yes, yes, the carpet is fine.... Lickety-spit, I don't have all day."

She twirled her wand, and I found myself suddenly cross-legged on the floor in between Amara and Blair.

"Such luck that I dropped into your class this morning." (We didn't think it was lucky!) "You see, it helped me make up my m nd about something. About time, too—with only TEN days to go."

Wait ... oh! We all started nudging each other.

"What I always say is that it's very important that—"

"*The trip must be right for the witches and the witches must be right for the trip?*" Winnie was too excited to remember not to interrupt.

"Exactly so! And that's why I'm happy to tell you that we're off to **Cadabra Castle**!"

Everyone immediately started chattering among themselves.

Ms. Sparks put up her hand for silence. "Trips to **Cadabra** are very rare, but I have no doubt you will all benefit from the particular classes you will have there."

"*Classes?*" Izzi sounded shocked. "There are going to be CLASSES?"

Ms. Sparks laughed. "Oh yes, indeed there are! Did you think this was going to be a *vacation?*" (Most of the class are nodding.) "Not quite like the classes you're used to, but a lot of learning and—"

"*You're sitting on my cloak,*" hissed Blair, tugging at it until I practically tumbled into Amara's lap.

"*Bonding!*" finished Ms. Sparks, raising an eyebrow and looking in our direction. "You are a wonderful and very *enthusiastic* group, but from what I've seen, and from what your teachers tell me, it's high time you all improved your teamwork skills, and there's nowhere better than **Cadabra** for that!"

Her voice became more serious. "Faced with the special challenges of the castle and the wilderness that surrounds it, you may well find you need to rely on one another a little more than usual and certainly listen to one another more than you did in Miss Lupo's class this morning! Now I need each of you to ask your responsible grown-up to sign a permission slip."

A single twitch of her wand and a letter dropped into each of our suddenly outstretched hands.

"Pop it into the cauldron by Mrs. Slater's desk and it will reach me. Not that I expect anyone to check the 'NO' box! After all, I'll *probably* bring you all back in one piece."

Eeeeeeeek!!

4:55 p.m. Home

Things I now know about Cadabra Castle

- Winnie says that in the olden days it was the home of the very first WITCH SCHOOL, ever!
- Dr. Pellicano says that the castle is hidden in a DEEP AND DARK WILDERNESS and that we'd better start paying attention in geography if we don't want to get lost and stuck there for a HUNDRED years.*
- Blair says it's where they invented the rules of **GO**.
- Puck says he's heard that the food is amazing (hopefully, not witch sausages).

And ....
- It's HAUNTED!!!

That last one might not be true because Hunter said it and he tells a lot of fibs. *Fingers crossed!*

"You **toadbrains** know all about the ghost,

---

*I would NOT like that!

right?" he shouted as we were all walking down the driveway after school.

"*Ghost?*" breathed Polly, her eyes almost popping out of her head.

"Yeah, GHOST!" Hunter added some *wooo-wooo* noises that would have been scarier if he hadn't been stuffing his face with fluffmallows at the same time. "It's TEN times as tall as a normal person, with two heads and red eyes. The famous ghost of **Cadabra**, *Principal Maggitty Crawe*."

"*I* know all about it," boasted Izzi. "I've heard it's TWENTY times as tall as a normal person and only seen at midnight when there's a full moon and—"

Polly looked as panicky as if an actual ghost were standing right in front of her.

Puck shot a look at her and said, "One of my moms went to **Cadabra** when she was in eighth grade and she never said anything about a ghost. I'm sure she would have if she'd seen one because it's not the kind of thing you forget to mention—even if it only has *one* head."

Polly let out the biggest *PHEW* I'd ever heard.

"EXCEPT MY DAD *SAW* HIM!" bellowed Hunter. "WITH HIS OWN EYES!"

There was a long silence broken only by a nervy-squeak from Polly. Not even Blair said anything.

I gave myself a shake and began to say, "There's no such thing as *gh*—" But then I remembered that once upon a time, not very long ago, I'd thought there was no such thing as *witches*....

5:30 p.m. Home

Have been thinking about it and have decided that witches are one thing and ghosts are quite another. I am ~~one hundred~~ ~~ninety-nine~~ ninety-one percent certain I don't believe in them.

6:33 p.m.

"Can I go?" I ask bravely, handing Dad the permission slip.

"Well...." He hesitates. "I've never heard of **Cadabra**. Let's see if we can find it on one of my maps."

8:45 p.m.

It took forever, but we've found it! Well, Stan found it, really—hopping up and down on one of the pages of an old atlas and croaking until we paid attention to him.

"**Cadabra Castle**! Well, well, it really is in the middle of nowhere! Looks like there's a forest and marshland and there's something else...." Dad points at what looks like a witch's-hat shape on the page. "Odd. I don't know that symbol."

"Probably a stain," I say quickly. "How far away is it?" I ask, turning the map every which way for a clue.

"I'd say about one hundred and fifty miles." Dad

doesn't seem to find maps almost as confusing as I do. "As the crow flies. But you're not a crow, hahahaha!"

I'm more like a crow than he knows. Everyone says we'll be flying there. ONE HUNDRED AND FIFTY MILES!! *Gulp, that's a long way from home.*

"Should— I mean *can* I go?"

"Of course you can. Hand me a pen, Bea."

Too late to back out now—I'm going to **Cadabra**!

10:03 p.m.
Even if I did believe in ghosts—which I ~~ninety-one~~ **definitely much more than fifty percent** *don't*—I'm not scared of them. I mean they're probably mostly friendly, right?

Midnight
Thunder and lightning!

On second thought, maybe I am a *tiny* bit scared of ghosts.

SATURDAY, JANUARY 8

4:01 p.m. Home

Ash and Amara have come over to hang out.

"Everyone always says old castles are haunted," Ash scoffs when we tell him about **Cadabra**. "It's not true. It's just to attract tourists."

"I don't think they WANT tourists to come to **Cadabra**," says Amara. "It's a *witch* castle."

"Well, you don't actually believe in ghosts, do you?" he asks us.

"*Noooooo*. Course not ... well, *probably* not," I babble.

Ash starts explaining why it's scientifically IMPOSSIBLE for ghosts to exist, but neither of us can understand what he's saying and Amara loses interest and goes to root in the cupboard for something to eat.

"What's this?" she asks, nudging a teetering tower of scribbled-over pages to make room for cookies.

"Dad's book," I say. "It's all about the weather in Little Spellshire. He hasn't finished writing it yet."

"'*The temperature can change from frosty to scorching in a matter of seconds...,*'" Amara reads aloud. "Well, we all know that."

"Yes, but Dad wants to explain it to people who don't live here," I say proudly. "You know, people who are especially interested in weird weather. That's why we moved here—so he could write it."

"But, Bea...." Amara looks worried. "If that's the only reason you came here, what happens when he finishes it?"

"What?"

Now Ash is looking worried. *Really* worried....

Oh!

Oh, NO! This is WAY scarier than any ghost....

If Dad and I only moved to Little Spellshire so he could write this book, would we move AWAY from Little Spellshire when he finishes it?

4:45 p.m.

Sent Ash and Amara home so I could concentrate on WORRYING. I do my best worrying on my own.

4:50 p.m.

Not completely on my own ... *Stan!* I couldn't ever leave Stan.

5:00 p.m.

How long does it take to write a book??

5:34 p.m.

Dad's just come in from the yard, talking about the wonders of thunder-snow.

"Never mind that!" I say. "How much of your book have you written?"

He looks a bit surprised at me asking. "Well, you know what writing books is like." (*No, no, I don't!*) "Very hard to tell how it's going when you're in the middle of it. It's driving me bananas."

He tugs at his hair like he wants to pull it out and adds, "I suppose one way or another I'll *have* to finish it soon and I promise you this, Bea, the next book I write will be about something easier to explain than the weather in Little Spellshire!"

Nooooooooo!

10:32 p.m.
Lying awake, doing a bit more panicking. I need a PLAN....

Midnight
Wait.... If Dad never finishes this book, then we'll never leave Little Spellshire, right?

I am a GENIUS.

SUNDAY, JANUARY 9

5:43 p.m. Home

Instead of going swimming in Cauldron Pond with my friends, I stayed at home all day, following Dad around, *getting in his way* and asking him a ton of random questions. It was very annoying for both of us.

"Oh, dear," says Dad, "I haven't written a thing today."

My cunning plan is working!

Why don't humans have tails?

What's the best thing to do if attacked by a bear?

How did crocodiles survive the meteor when dinosaurs didn't?

MONDAY, JANUARY 10

8:50 a.m. School

"I was worried for a minute that my dad wasn't going to let me go to **Cadabra**," says Fabi, dropping his signed permission slip into the cauldron by Mrs. Slater's desk. "He said he still has nightmares about his trip there."

"Because he saw the TWO-H-H-HEADED g-gh-ghost?" asks Polly, clutching her hands so tightly together she's leaving nail marks.

"No, but he told me he heard *noises* and that was enough for him. But then my grandma said he was being ridiculous and wibble-bottomed and that she'd had the best week of her life at **Cadabra**." Fabi grins. "I can't wait. I'd love to meet a ghost."

"*My dad saw it THIRTEEN TIMES and it was TERRIFYING!*" bellows Hunter.

Winnie glares at him. "There is no reliable evidence of a ghost at **Cadabra**," she says firmly, pulling Polly gently away from the cauldron before she can fish her permission slip out again.

"*My dad—*"

"There have been a number of *alleged* sightings," interrupts Winnie, shooting Hunter the kind of *do-not-interrupt-me* look Miss Lupo specializes in, "but nothing's been proven."

"Those alleged sightings," asks Izzi, "were they of a ten-times-human-sized ghost with two heads ... or possibly *no* head at all, called Principal Maggitty Crawe?"

Winnie ignores her, gives Polly's arm a reassuring pat, and says, "There's almost certainly NO GHOST AT ALL."

"OR maybe there are A BUNCH of ghosts—hiding in the dungeons, haunting the toilets, roaming the battlements. Sneaking up on you.... BOO!"

Hunter makes everyone jump, but most of us are laughing. Except for Polly. And Blair.

"*I'm* not scared of ghosts," she says fiercely, even though no one said she was.

8:55 a.m.

I think if I were ever to meet a ghost I'd rather not meet it in a toilet.*

9:10 a.m.

Mr. Muddy isn't coming on the school trip with us, and oddly, he doesn't seem disappointed AT ALL.

"I'll miss you all, of course, but the seventh graders aren't going to teach themselves and anyway—"

---

*Which I'm sure I won't because I probably don't believe in them.

he grins—"one visit to **Cadabra** was probably enough for me."

"Is it because you're scared of ghosts, sir?" asks Hunter.

"What I'm scared of," said Mr. Muddy, looking at his watch, "is what Miss Lupo will say if you all are late for chemistry again."

10:13 a.m.

Miss Lupo says that if she hears ONE. MORE. WORD about the school trip while we're supposed to be concentrating on the healing power of squashed jelly ears, she will turn us all into mushrooms.

Homework: Draw and label a jelly ear and one other fungus of your choice.

11:21 a.m.

For some reason, Mr. Smith thinks we'll need all our best measuring skills at **Cadabra** so he's given us a "fun test" on inches.

2:11 p.m.

Professor Crisp is coming with us to **Cadabra**!

"Ah, I can't wait to go back," he says, smiling so widely I worry his papery old face might split. "There's no better place to learn about our history than the castle where so much of it happened."

He starts pulling out ancient books from the shelves behind him, dislodging clouds of dust and a small hedgehog.

"Please, sir!" calls out Puck. "You're *very old*, so you'll know—is there a ghost at **Cadabra**?"

"Is it ten times the size of a normal person—"

"TWENTY times—"

CRASH! Everyone jumps, but it's only Blair—somehow she's managed to knock over a cauldron. The questions start again.

"Is it headless?"

"Does it have FIVE heads?"

Everyone is shouting questions at once, and Professor Crisp has to wave his wand for silence.

"So I see you've heard the stories about Princpial Maggitty Crawe then," he says with a chuckle.

"*Is he real?*" I ask, (carefully) cuddling the hedgehog that's climbed into my lap.

"He *was* very real. As real as you, or me, or that hedgehog there. And no, he didn't have five heads or no heads, and as far as I know he was a perfectly normal height. Very important man, Principal Crawe—the first princpial of the very first witch school in the land."

"But is he a *GHOST*?" Hunter is not giving up.

Professor Crisp shrugs. "I can't answer that." He ignores all our moans of protest and says, "But I *can* tell you all about the witches' stone circle at Stonehenge. If you're all sitting comfortably, I shall begin."

6:00 p.m. Home

Have asked Dad to help me with my math after dinner. I'll do ANYTHING to stop him from working on his book.

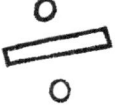

TUESDAY, JANUARY 11

9:25 a.m. School
"FIRE!" yells Mr. Muddy, and we all look around in a panic before we realize he's talking about today's class. "How to start one."

He flicks his wand, mutters something, and the contents of the garbage can (mostly our homework) bursts into flames.

"You never know when you might be in need of a bit of crackly-cozy comfort ... especially when you're far from home."*

10:35 a.m.
The good news is that I haven't set fire to myself. The bad news is that I *have* set fire to Puck's cloak

*Like, 150 MILES away?!!!

and now Mr. Muddy has made it rain and everyone's wet and angry.

3:23 p.m.
Final score:

| DODOS: 21 | | DRAGONS: 22 |

"Good game!" shouts Ms. Celery once we've all dismounted. "I must say, Blair and Bea, you two are shaping up to be a fine **GO** rivalry."

I look sadly at the score—a rivalry I was losing.

"Or maybe I should try you out on the same team. What do you think?"

Blair and I exchange such a look of HORROR that everyone bursts out laughing. Maybe NOT.

"Will we be able to play **GO** at Cadabra?" asks Fabi.

"No," says Ms. Celery.

Broomsticks! "Why not?"

"Because the Great **GO** Chimney of Cadabra fell down in 1721." Ms. Celery looks as upset as if it had happened yesterday. "Besides, I'm not sure I'd trust all of you to make it to the end of a game ALIVE without me to referee— Puck Berry, get down from that roof THIS INSTANT!"

She waits for him to crash-land in a nearby bush and goes on. "In fact, now that I think about it, it would be a very good idea if you were all to practice the Spiky-Treetop-Dodge."

4:10 p.m. Home

And so we did and now I'm now covered in pine needles like a porcupine.

6.30 p.m.

"Have you seen my lucky pen?"
Dad's in a panic. "I've been looking for it all day. You know I can't work without it!"

I shake my head and cross my fingers behind my back. (I've planted it in the yard under the clump of toadflax. I think my plan's going very well.)

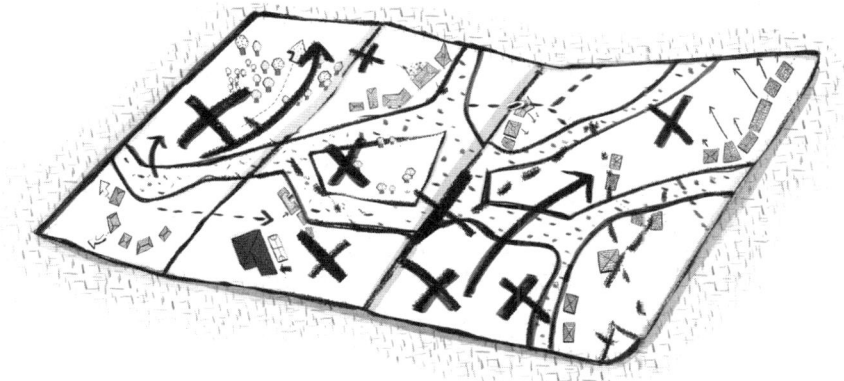

WEDNESDAY, JANUARY 12

9:20 a.m. School

Our geography lesson is outside today.

"Basic land-navigation skills," says Dr. Pellicano, handing each of us a big map of the school grounds. "Very simple. Just read the map and follow the route marked out from here—" she jabs the page—"to there."

She makes it sound so easy, but even when I manage to stop my map from blowing around in the wind, it mostly looks like squiggles to me. How are we meant to "read" *squiggles*?

"Excuse me, Dr. Pellicano?" Winnie sticks her hand up. "What are all the big red Xs?"

"They mark the spot where WITCH-EATING

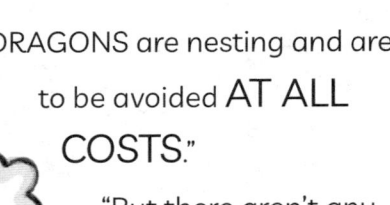

DRAGONS are nesting and are to be avoided AT ALL COSTS."

"But there aren't any witch-eating dragons on the school grounds."

"This morning," Dr. Pellicano replies firmly, "for the purposes of this lesson, there *are*." *Gulp!!* "The Xs mark areas of the grounds that we are going to imagine are mortally dangerous and universally deadly. You are going to avoid them by READING YOUR MAPS. If you fail to avoid them, you will be OUT. Am I understood?"

Um … not really. "But the dragons aren't *actually, really, literally* there, are they?" I ask.

"No." Dr. Pellicano sighs sadly. "Ms. Sparks said I wasn't allowed."

10:03 a.m.

Fabi, Puck, Amara, and me are all OUT already and that means extra geography homework for us. SIGH.

Geography homework:
Draw a map of your own backyard from a bird's-eye view (you may find this easier to do from your broomstick). Watch out for any dragon nests!

4:35 p.m. Taffy Tallywick's Teashop

It was Winnie's idea to go to Taffy's after school for a pre-trip planning meeting. She says we're all spending too much time talking about silly things like ghosts and not enough time making lists.

"It's good to be prepared," she says, happily pulling a clipboard out of her schoolbag. Cadabra— FORWARD PLANNING. "Item one—have you all finished your packing?"

That would be a NO* from me and Amcra and Fabi and Puck.

Winnie rolls her eyes and makes us all copy down a list of extra things we'll need fluffmallows, cookies, lots of witchy snacks for them and chips for me, fizzy skullsquigglers, notebooks (diary for me), etc. etc.

*Haven't even started!

"Item two—teams. Ms. Sparks says there will be team building so we have to be prepared." She starts writing down our names. "I'll put a little asterisk beside mine so everyone knows I'm in charge of organizing."

Ribbit!

"What about Stan?" I ask, pouring some water into a saucer for him to paddle in.

"*Obviously*, Stan is on our team," they all chorus.

"But I don't think he should be in charge," says Winnie quite reasonably. "Does he have a surname? No?"

We watch as she neatly writes Mr. Stan on her list.

"Speaking of names.... Item three—team name."

5:32 p.m.

Have eaten so many triple-chocolate cookies I feel a little sick, but we've got a name ... Team Finkelspark! Still a bit ~~appryhensiv~~ worried about what might happen on this witch trip but it's nice to be part of a team!

The Extraordinary: Spring Semester Issue 1

Sports News and Notices

- Congratulations to the tenth-grade Flying Cauldrons who, in a school record, managed to get through an entire match without a single foul.

- Ms. Celery would like to warn all **GOers** that if they show up late to the pitches they WILL be made to run (NOT FLY) up and down the school driveway until they beg for mercy.

Other Notices

- The toads that visit the plant pots outside the principal's office are, by nature, rather shy. Students are requested to leave them in peace.

Quick-fire Q & A with Dr. Pellicano!

Q: Favorite place on Earth?

A: That's a ridiculous question, but I am a very busy witch and this is meant to be "quick-fire"—so let's say Patagonia.

Q: Favorite pet?

A: When I was younger and doing a lot of mountain trekking, I had a close relationship with a yak named Yakshap. I would never have called him a pet as that would have affronted his dignity. Yaks have a great deal of dignity. I am also always accompanied on my travels by a rock that I call Eclogite (because that is its correct name). I find my rock more intelligent than most people I meet.

Q: Favorite joke?

A: I prefer facts.

Um ... thank you, Dr. Pellicano!

Dear Agony Witch

Dear Agony Witch,

I am going on my first residential witch-school trip this semester and I am nervous about being away from home in a strange place. I don't want to tell anyone in case they laugh at me. Do you have any advice?

Love,

A Secretly Worried New-Witch

Dear ~~Be~~ Secretly Worried New-Witch,

I'm sure a lot of your friends are secretly worried about being homesick, too! I can't guarantee you won't miss home a tiny bit, but you will be so busy having adventures that the time will FLY. I'd advise you to pack something special to remind you of home, and don't forget that missive powder!

Love,

Agony Witch x

FRIDAY, JANUARY 14

9:25 a.m. School

"Don't think for one second that I won't be expecting you to keep up your potions work while you're away," says Miss Lupo sternly. "The wilderness around **Cadabra Castle** is rich in ingredients for healing recipes. What I want you—" She breaks off and yells, "Puck Berry! Bloodwort is NOT meant to go up your nose."

"AAAAACHOOOO!"

9:33 a.m.

"As I was saying," says Miss Lupo when Puck eventually stops sneezing, "what I want you to do while you're away is to collect specimens of as many of the following healing plants as you can and bring them back to school." She clicks her fingers, and a list starts to write itself on the wall behind her.

Scrooby grass
Piggy-toe leaves
Devil's garters

"I hope these aren't going into a drink-me potion," mutters Blair, but Miss Lupo ignores her and lectures us for five whole minutes on the anti-swelling properties of piggy-toe leaves. The list keeps getting longer.

Cauliflower fungus
Jelly ear fungus

"Do you know any anti-ghost potions?" asks Blair.
"No such thing," says Miss Lupo merrily.
Oh, dear!

11:27 a.m.

Madam Binx is making us work extra hard on our healing charms today. "Fungi are all very well and good," she says, "but if you really want to unlock their medicinal magic, you need to learn the right rhymes."

11:59 a.m.

It's the end of the class, and I've only managed to learn the first two lines of a very long chant....

> I'm cut and bruised, oh woe and DOOM.
> Help me, please, oh kind MUSHROOM!

2:40 p.m.

The Friday Lecture was all about Dr. Pellicano's trip to study ice crystals in the Dark Star labyrinth in Uzbekistan.

"Weren't you scared?" asked Amara at question time.

"Of course she wasn't!" shouted Hunter.

"Actually, *yes*, I was," said Dr. Pellicano. "*Very* scared. It's very, very deep and very, very dark and very, *very* hard to find your way around. But I was part of a team of witch geographers, and we all watched out for one another. It's perfectly normal to be scared sometimes. Anyway, I was also curious and interested. It *is* possible to feel more than one thing at the same time, you know."

If you ask me, it's perfectly normal to be scared of Dr. Pellicano, but I have to admit she does have a lot of good stories to tell.

6:25 p.m. Home

The school gave us a packing list for the trip and I should have known better than to check it in the kitchen. Most of it was ordinary (cozy sweaters/pajamas/shirts/pants, etc.) but some of it was more *unusual*....

"One week's supply of *missive powder*? What on Earth is that?" asks Dad, leaning over my shoulder to read before I can stop him.

I have NO IDEA, but Winnie has promised to bring me some over tomorrow so I guess I'll find out then. Luckily, before Dad can ask any more awkward questions, the phone starts ringing.

6:36 p.m.
It was my grandma, and after I'd filled her in on everything non-witchy I'd been doing, I passed her over to Dad and listened to him telling her all about yesterday's sudden storm of red hailstones and Monday's very peculiar shower of toads. It's amazing how long some grown-ups can spend talking about the weather.

"I can't make scientific sense of any of it," Dad groans. "I wish I'd never agreed to write a book about it! ... What's that? ... Come back to Milton Keynes to write the next one? Hahaha! ... Lots of sensible weather in Milton Keynes to write about? Haha! Maybe I should! Haha!"

Go back to Milton Keynes?! This is SO not funny....

SATURDAY, JANUARY 15

4:11 p.m. Home

Just back from a shopping expedition with Dad and I don't know what to do.

Little Spellshire was looking its loveliest best. The sun was shining and the birds were tweeting and the UnCommon was dotted with slinky black cats washing their paws and looking pleased with themselves. Everyone seemed to be in a good mood. I might be imagining it, but since Ms. Sparks invited the **Academy** students to the Extraordinary sports day last semester, it does feel like there's a friendlier atmosphere between the non-witches and the witches in town. But all I could think about was how SAD I would be if I ever had to live anywhere else.

One way or another, I had to stop Dad from finishing that book!

"Can we stop off at Taffy's for cake?" I tugged him to a halt in front of the teashop.

"I really should get back and do some work...."

He hesitated, but luckily Taffy—carrying a freshly baked chocolate cake on a big platter—saw us and waved through the steamy window.

"Good idea!" he agreed, waving back. "After all, I'll have plenty of time to catch up on my writing when you're away. All that wonderful peace and quiet."

Nooooooo! There's a **Cadabra**-shaped HOLE in my plan!

5:42 p.m.

I still don't know what to do, but I'm very distracted because Winnie and Amara and Puck have brought over the missive powder and I'm not sure what I was expecting, but not this. It's just as well that Dad's working in the shed because this would be very hard to explain.

"Here," said Puck, handing me a tiny lidded cauldron. "Don't spill it," he warned.

Very carefully, with everyone watching (Ash had come over to join us, too), I pried open the lid.... Inside, there was what looked like *gold dust*.

"What do I do with it?"

"I'll show you." Winnie grabbed some paper and a pen and scribbled:

Dear Bea,
THIS is what missive powder is for.
Lots of love xx

Then she folded the paper into the shape of a *tiny broomstick* and wrote on the back in mouse-sized handwriting:

To Miss Bea Black
1 Piggoty Lane
First-floor bedroom (second door when you turn left at the top of the stairs)

And then she carefully took a pinch of dust out of the mini-cauldron and sprinkled it on the note. There was a burst of multicolored sparks ... a **WHOOSH** and—

"Where did it *go*?" I gasped.

"Follow Stan!" Amara giggled and pointed at my frog, who was hopping toward the stairs as fast as I've ever seen him move!

Seconds later, I crashed into my bedroom and—**SWOOSH**—I was practically hit on the nose by a tiny paper broomstick!

Dragons!

6:00 p.m.

"It's witch-to-witch messaging in super-quick time."

I'm back in the kitchen and Winnie is explaining. "Perfect for school trips—if we need to get in touch with home, then we can. Simple."

For a second, I feel a big rush of relief and then I realize ... witch-to-*witch* messaging....

"It's not simple for *me*, though, is it? I won't be able to send a message to my dad." (Would there even be a *phone* at **Cadabra**?) "What if he's lonely without me?"* I *knew* we should have gotten a dog.

And then, all in a rush, the thing I'm most worrying about bursts out. "*What if he makes the most of all the peace and quiet to finish his book and then we have to leave here—*" there's a gasp from the others—"*and move somewhere else with no witches or frogs or* **GO***, like the Galápagos or MILTON KEYNES, so he can write a new book about weather-that-makes-scientific-sense and—*"

"Whoa, slow down, Bea!" commands Winnie.

"*Breathe*," suggests Amara gently. "Your face has turned all red."

That's because I'm trying very hard not to cry.

*Or I'M lonely without him!

"You should talk to him," says Winnie in her most sensible voice.

And risk him saying we had to go? *Noooooo!* I blink away my tears and shake my head firmly. "I have a better idea—I'm going to make sure he *never* finishes it." And I tell them all about my cunning plan. I really am a genius. Except for one thing....

"*But what am I going to do when I'm away at* **Cadabra**? Maybe I should stay at home."

More horrified gasps.

"Okay, okay, don't panic, Bea. I'll keep an eye on your dad," says Ash gruffly. "*I'll* make sure he doesn't get any peace and quiet to finish his book."

"But I'll be so far away and I won't know what's happening...." I pause. "Unless...."

"Unless *what*?"

"Unless...."

No. I *can't* ask Ash to do magic. It didn't go well last time* and I *promised* I'd never ask him to try again.

---

*Ash says he almost DIED, but that is ~~an eggsajer~~ not true.

"Nothing, never mind," I mumble.

"*Unless* –" he takes a deep breath—"I try and do missives, too."

"But you said—"

"That I'd never do magic again?"

I nod.

"Well...." He takes another deep breath. "I think I'm going to have to make an exception because this is an *emergency*."

He's being so nice that I almost get teary again, but instead I give him a squashy hug (and my last fluffmallow, which I think he prefers).

9:35 p.m.

Ash is definitely one of the top three reasons* why I CAN'T leave Little Spellshire.

9:55 p.m.

Feeling much better about the trip again. I'm *almost* more excited than nervous!

---

*Ash, Stan, and ALL my witchy friends, and Excalibur the miniature pig, and even the teachers, and.... Ahhhhh, there are a GAZILLION reasons!

SUNDAY, JANUARY 16 (SCHOOL TRIP EVE!)

6:01 p.m. Home

Packing's finished AT LAST.

Dad's been racing around in circles all day like a dog chasing its tail, occasionally barking questions at me. "Did you remember to pack Band Aids?"

"Yes." (One packet of Miss Lupo's Extraordinary Band Aids that smell like pickled onions and one packet of ordinary ones that don't smell like anything.)

"Did you remember to pack cozy shirts?"

"Yes." (No.)

"I should make you a packed lunch for the bus trip." Dad peers hopefully into the fridge, which is empty except for half a tin of sardines and a jar of marmalade.

"No need!" I say quickly. "The school's doing it."
I ram some more packets of chips into my bag while he's not looking. "Anyway, I don't think we'll be going by bus." I hide a grin.

"Train?"

Obviously, I can't say BROOMSTICKS so I pretend I haven't heard him.

"Are you sure you want to take Stan with you?" Dad asks.

"Of course I do!"

I've made him a travel pouch out of an old sock so that he'll be safe on the broom ride. It will be a **Great Froggy Adventure**.

"I'm going to miss Stan."

"What about ME, Dad?"

Dad grins and pulls me into a hug. "And you!"

10:03 p.m.

Stan's snoring, but I'm too nervy-excited to sleep!

*He'll do his froggy best to stop me from feeling homesick!!

MONDAY, JANUARY 17 (TODAY'S THE DAY!)

5:33 a.m. Home

Woke up in a panic thinking I'd overslept and everyone had left without me.

8:43 a.m.

Ash came over on his way to school to exchange some cookies his mom had made me for my journey for some missive powder.

"Message me when you get there," he whispers with a grin. "*And don't worry about your dad. I've got this!*"

11:03 a.m.

"Are you sure I can't come and wave you off?" said Dad after we'd eaten most of the cookies for breakfast. "I'd like to."

I'd like that, too, but I couldn't risk it.

"Ms. Sparks said we have to leave our responsible grown-ups at home," I fibbed. "Um ... it's to avoid any emotional farewells."

And then I flew across the room* and gave him the hardest, longest hug, and he said all the sensible things he'd said ten times already about being well behaved and careful and not staying up late *blah blah*, and then he said a lot of silly things about how Stan will have to kiss me good night for him and how I must remember to wear cozy pants.

I'll TRY not to worry about him, but I'm definitely going to miss him!

*Not literally.

12:23 p.m. School gates

We haven't even set off and nobody's happy....

"*EEEEEUGH!*" I could hear Blair before I even reached the gates. "NO WAY!"

And it didn't take long for me to see what she was upset about. Half hidden by a tangle of spiky holly bushes was the shabbiest, oldest, ugliest, orangey-est BUS I had ever seen in my life.

"We can't travel in *that*," Izzi sputtered.

Mr. Muddy (who'd shown up with a few of the other teachers as well as some witchy grown-ups to wave us off) silently pointed at a board taped to the side of the bus.

"B-but what about flying?" Puck sounded as shocked as I felt.

"Oh, what a good idea!" said Dr. Pellicano sarcastically, materializing beside us with a puff of smoke. "Nothing like a whole class of badly behaved witches and a frog with basic broom skills* flying overhead for keeping the secret."

"Those of us who know, *know*—" began Mr. Muddy.

"And those of them who don't, *can't*," we all finished miserably.

"But last year they flew to the Bottomless Fairy Pools," Amara pointed out.

"That's not almost as far away, and anyway, it was a terrible mistake," said Mr. Muddy sadly. "There were six crashes and we had to befuddle several Ordinaries."

"We could fly at nighttime," I suggested, and everyone (except Winnie) nodded enthusiastically.

"*Pffff!*" said Dr. Pellicano. "I wouldn't trust you children on a night flight around my backyard."

"MY DAD said they flew to **Cadabra** overnight on

---

*I don't think Stan has ANY broom skills.

their school trip. IT'S NOT FAIR!" bellowed Hunter.

"I remember!" Professor Crisp shuddered. "A near-death experience for us all! *Never again.* Traveling by wheels will be much safer."

One of the mudguards fell off the bus and rolled along the road toward us.

Izzi started moaning. "I'm going to be bus sick," she wailed.

"There, there," said her mom, handing her a gnarly knob of ginger to chew on. "Honestly, couldn't the school have found something better?"

"Maybe an enchanted pumpkin coach?" I *think* Winnie was joking.

"With six mice coachmen, I suppose." Blair was *definitely* being sarcastic.

"We did consider that option," said Professor Crisp, "but we think you'll like this better. A less cramped, smoother ride."

"It's just *Ordinary*." I squashed my nerves firmly and added, "It'll be fun—we can play I Spy all the way there."

"What's I Spy?" asked Winnie.

I grinned—I liked it when I got to teach them something new instead of the other way around. "It's a game we—"

"*Eeeugh*. I don't want to learn *Ordinary* games on an *Ordinary* bus." Blair was glaring at me like everything was *my* fault.

"Blair and Bea, *please*, for once may we have a little harmony!" Ms. Sparks made a neat broomstick landing beside us. "Today isn't a day for squabbling. It's a day for sharing a magnificent adventure." She looked at the bus and beamed. "Isn't she gorgeous? So *orange!*"

1:03 p.m. On the bus!

Hunter and Izzi and Blair might never have been on an Ordinary bus before, but they still managed to claim the back seat. I slid in next to Winnie and looked across her out of the window at all the waving witches shouting things like: "Send us a missive as soon as you arrive!" (the parents) and, "Watch out for wolfwishes!" (Professor Agu) and, "Don't forget the jelly ears!" (Miss Lupo).

"Buckle up, witches!" shouts Professor Crisp from the driver's seat.

We're off!

3:03 p.m. Somewhere between Little Spellshire and Cadabra

We've been driving for two whole hours, and Winnie says we're still not even halfway there. This bus—which kind of hops along like a confused frog—is very slow.

Our packed lunch—witch sausage rolls (chips for me) and brownies—seems *forever* ago and we're on what feels like the millionth round of I Spy.

"I spy something beginning with Z," I begin. Zephyr rolls her eyes at me and slinks down from Ms. Sparks's lap into her extra-large handbag. "Um … forget that! I spy something beginning with F."

"Fabi!" shouts Amara just as Puck swallows the last fluffmallow.

4:01 p.m.
Playing Two Truths and a Lie with witches is IMPOSSIBLE—how was I supposed to know that Blair *did* levitate her baby sister onto the sports pavilion roof, but had never eaten a potato?

4:11 p.m. STILL somewhere between Little Spellshire and Cadabra
We've been on this bus for a hundred years.*

"Are we almost there yet?" asks Izzi.

"No," says Dr. Pellicano.

4:14 p.m.
"Are we almost there yet?" asks Puck.

"No," says Dr. Pellicano.

*Approximately.

4:19 p.m.

"Are we almost there yet?" asks Polly and Flame and Blair and Li and Raven and Fabi and Amara and everyone else and me.

"No!" says Dr. Pellicano. "And I shall turn the next person who asks into a FUNGUS BEETLE."

5:32 p.m. Can't believe this, but we're STILL on the bus

I now know ALL the verses to the Extraordinary school chant (including the unofficial one that's rude about the teachers).

"THIS IS THE MOST BORINGEST JOURNEY IN THE HISTORY OF BORING BUS JOURNEYS!" bellows Hunter from the back.

Ms. Sparks turns around in her seat and stares at him. "*Really?*" She sounds genuinely surprised. "I've found it most interesting." The other teachers (and Zephyr) nod. "You should have said something."

She flicks her wand, and in an instant the bus is full of *BUBBLES*!

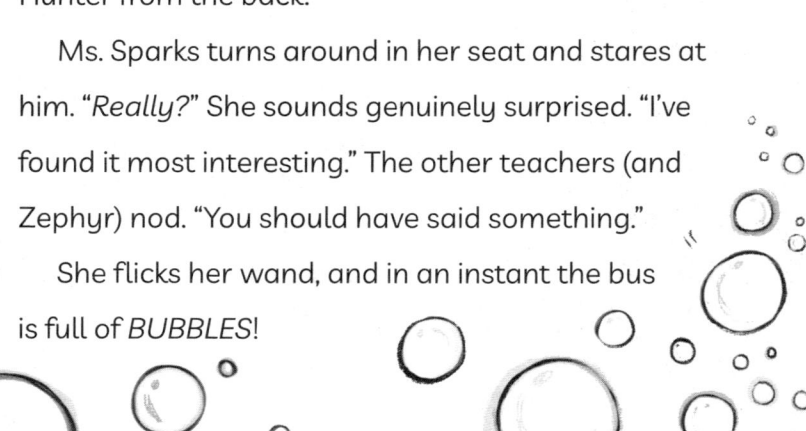

"I could have made it so much more extraordinary! Ah, well, too late now," she says just as the bus *swerves* (sadly popping most of the bubbles).

Now we're on some kind of narrow road tented over with shaggy trees. It's already dark, but in the light of the bus's headlights, I can see two crumbling stone pillars topped with statues of oversized ravens.

"Tight squeeze!" shouts the professor. "Breathe in, witches!"

Caw! Caw! Caw!

Eeeek, maybe they weren't statues! The huge ravens are swooping and diving past the windows as the bus hops and stalls through the pillars and down a potholed path.

"I feel sick!" wails Izzi, but everyone ignores her because, with a *screeeeeech* of the brakes, we're grinding to a halt.

"ARE WE HERE?"

"WHY HAVE WE STOPPED?"

"IS THIS **CADABRA**?"

"I NEED THE BATHROOM!"

"WHERE'S THE CASTLE?"

Everyone's shouting.

I can't see the castle, but the teachers are summoning the luggage down from the racks and flicking their capes over their shoulders....
I think we've arrived!!
I'm BURSTING with nervy-excitement!!

6:11 p.m. In a clearing (hopefully near Cadabra Castle)

We have NOT arrived.

I STILL can't see the castle, and the excitement is wearing off* because we've had to *walk* in the dark through trees for what feels like forever. And I'm WET. I now know that the reason the bus couldn't go any farther was because it couldn't cross the bridge, and I now also know that's because there is basically *no bridge left at all*, just some mossy stones with a couple

*But NOT the nerves!

of slimy, creaky planks balanced between them. It's amazing* that I was the only witch to fall in.

6:35 p.m.

"*LOOK!*" cries Fabi.

The moon is slipping out from behind some clouds and rising up in front of us—*really close*— s....

Um ... A BIG PILE OF RUINS.

Nothing more than a huge mound of toppled-over stones and two or three jagged walls that look like they might once have belonged to towers. It's not what I'd call a *castle*. There's a big sign saying: **KEEP OUT—DANGER.** *Oh, no!*

"Where are we going to—"

"*LOOOOOOOOOK!*" cries Fabi again.

6:37 p.m.

Something VERY peculiar is going on.... The stones are *shimmering* and *glimmering* and *rearranging themselves*. They're ... GROWING???

*TYPICAL (also embarrassing...).

6:40 p.m.

"How the—?"

"What the—?"

"That's better! Dear old **Cadabra** revealed in all its glory." Ms. Sparks gives a little cheer and tucks her wand away. "Don't look so shocked," she says, turning to us all and laughing.

"But where did it—?"

"Come from? Oh, it was here all along—just hiding behind a Nothing-To-See-Here-But-A-Pile-Of-Old-Stones charm. Have none of you ever encountered one of those before?"

All of us—even Winnie—shake our heads and stare with our mouths open at...

THE CASTLE-IEST CASTLE I HAVE EVER SEEN.

It's also the SPOOKIEST castle I have ever seen. Even with the charm lifted, it's still partly in ruins. Every wall is covered in a thick layer of ivy, parts of the roof look like they've caved in, and two of the towers are as tumbledown as they were before.

Stan's seen enough—he hops down from his perch on my shoulder and snuggles down inside my hoodie. *Gulp.*

"Wait here, witches," says Ms. Sparks and flits off. Seconds later, she's swishing past the **KEEP OUT— DANGER** sign and rapping at the massive wooden door with her wand. She is so BRAVE!

Tat-tat-rat-a-tat….

CRREEEEAAK….

The door jolts open just a few inches and three bats and an owl fly out.

"Helloooooo, Dolly?" calls out Ms. Sparks and at once the door is flung open and a tiny and EXTREMELY old* witch springs out and pulls Ms. Sparks into a big hug!

"Ember! Can it really be you? And Zephyr! It is SO lovely to have you both back." Her high, silvery voice carries clearly in the still air. "Oooooh!" She peers over at us. "You've brought me some of your little witches. But don't they look *bedraggled*! The sooner we get you all inside, the better."

"Well?" Dr. Pellicano turns to us. "You heard Madam Pumpkin—what are you all waiting for?"

7:01 p.m. Cadabra Castle!!

The inside of this castle is even *castle-ier* (*good*) and even *spookier* (*BAD*) than the outside.

We're standing in an entrance hall so big we could play **GO** in it! It's very gloomy, lit only by a few

---

*Even older than Professor Crisp!

flickering candles, but I can see that the walls are hung with *gazillions* of witch hats and the ceiling is like a great upside-down boat with bats and owls snuggled into the big beams. The spiderwebs are the size of HAMMOCKS and it's *FREEZING* cold.

Broomsticks!

Madam Pumpkin has levitated herself onto a high table and is clapping her hands to get our attention.

"Welcome, witchlings! I'm Dolly and I've been taking care of **Cadabra Castle** for a VERY long time. There's nothing I love more than having visitors! This place really is much too big just for little old me and—"

She breaks off suddenly, pulls a wand out of her cardigan sleeve, and flicks it in the direction of a great carved fireplace. A second later, purple flames are leaping in the grate.

"There, that's a warmer welcome. What was I thinking, rattling on while you're all shivery?!

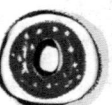

You're probably starving, too!"

Another flick of her wand and a big winged basket of warm doughnuts is making the rounds.

I think I like Dolly Pumpkin!

But we barely have time to thaw our frozen hands. "I mustn't keep you standing in the entrance hall," she says, "not when there's so much to see. Follow me. I'll take you on the grand tour."

7:10 p.m.

We're not getting much chance to see *anything* in this super-confusing whirlwind tour. Dolly is throwing open door after door at the speed of broomflight.

"Banquet hall," she trills, pointing to her right.

"Passage that leads down to the dungeons." She flings an arm to the left.

"Cloakroom. Visitors' borrow-a-broom room. Kitchens down those back stairs." She nods vaguely toward a closed door.

"Portrait galleries." She gestures in at least three different directions. "Bridge to the lower map room.

Underground passage to the Roman ruins."

My head is spinning.

At last she stops short by a door much smaller than the others. "Toilets," she announces.

There's a rush.

7:21 p.m.

By the time we all get back to the entrance hall (feeling *much* better), Dolly and the teachers are sitting around the fire, chatting like they're on vacation. We all make *shushing* faces at each other and try to creep close enough to eavesdrop.

"How you've grown, Ember!" says Dolly to Ms. Sparks. "And you, too, Trudi." She beams at Dr. Pellicano. "I remember *your* school trip like it was yesterday! The two of you—" Zephyr meows crossly— "the *three* of you getting up to all kinds of mischief!"

Imagining Dr. Pellicano and Ms. Sparks hanging out together is as hard as imagining me hanging out with Blair! But if Dr. Pellicano had been the kind of teacher that winked, I'd have thought she was winking at Ms. Sparks right then.

"I'll never forget that day when you—" Dolly turned around, saw us, and stopped short with a chuckle (just as she was getting to the interesting part!). "Now—" she looks at us and waves her arms skyward— "*somewhere* up there are your bedrooms, and at **Cadabra**, we always let you choose your own. So that might be something you want to get going with—"

7:51 p.m. Our Cadabra Castle bedroom!

She might as well have shouted, "Ready, set, go...."

It was WITCHY *PANDEEMONEEEUM* with everyone grabbing their friends and summoning their bags and pushing each other out of the way to get to the stairs.

"Follow me!" shouted Winnie to Amara and me, and—once we'd gotten over the surprise of seeing her run so fast—we did, up the stairs, then left, then right down a long, curving corridor.

"Winnie, hold on! Where are you going?"

"I don't have a clue!" Winnie leaned against a wall

to catch her breath. "I just know I don't want to end up in the dungeons or rooming with bats or worse … *with Izzi or Blair.*"

Good point! I grabbed her hand and Amara grabbed mine and we all ran together—around another corner, up another flight of stairs, then *another* until we found ourselves at the start of a long, straight corridor, so wide it was practically a room itself.

Every single inch of wall was covered in old portraits of witches in ruffs and witches in cloaks and witches in togas and witches in top hats!

"No time to stop and look," panted Winnie. "Let's just try all the doors."

There was a room filled right up to the ceiling with old cauldrons.

There was another room so stacked with piles of ancient books that we couldn't even get the door fully open. There were at least five locked doors.

There was a room covered in big, fat cobwebs, which Amara said looked cozy, but which I STRONGLY VETOED.

There was a strange bathroom with a toilet as big as a throne and a bath on claw feet.

And then there was only one door left to try—right at the end of the corridor, next to a larger than life-size*, dark, dusty portrait of an old beardy witch in a black gown with a HUGE white ruff. He was the sternest, gloomiest, crossest witch I had ever seen. He was *so* scary-looking that he made Dr. Pellicano look like a fluffmallow.

"Principal of Cadabra, 1537 to 1556, Maggitty Octavius Crawe," Amara said, reading the name engraved at the bottom of the portrait.

"MAGGITTY!" we all yelped and nervy-giggled and clutched each other. If I were ever going to meet a

*Or maybe he was just VERY TALL?

ghost, I definitely wouldn't want it to look like HIM!

Winnie was the first to calm down. "We can't be scared of a *picture* of a real, *live* human ... and a sweet little *cat*." She wiped off some of the dust with her sleeve so we could see.

She was right—a little black kitten was clinging by its claws to the end of one of Maggitty's bat-like cloak sleeves! It was very fluffy and sprinkled all over with tiny white star shapes, one eye was green, one eye was purple, and its paws were definitely too big for it. *Awwww!*

"Come on," said Winnie and reached out her hand to the curly door handle.... Finally, a room that wasn't dungeon-y, Blair-y, cauldron-y, spider-y, or (as far as we can tell) GHOST-Y!

It's shaped like a hexagon* and the walls are rough gray stone, but they're hung with faded tapestries and there's a huge fireplace covered in carved gargoyles. It is very dusty and more than a *little spooky*, but there is something very, VERY good about this room....

*Thank you, Mr. Smith!

It has a humongous four-poster bed!

Big enough for the three of us* to share, with green silk curtain-y things and piles of fluffy cushions and pillows that look like they'd be perfect for pillow fights and fort building. Things are looking up!

Amara flings herself onto the bed. "We are going to have SO MUCH FUN!" she shouts.

"*Hmmmmm.*" With a wave of her wand, Winnie lines up the bags neatly at the end of the bed, spells a crackling fire into life in the grate, and mutters a de-dustifying charm at the bookcase in the corner. "Right after we get this place cleaned up a little bit."

Guess that's my cue to stop scribbling!!

Span and spick, spick and span,
Wand, clean this room as best you can....

8:02 p.m.

Our room is cozier now. Stan thinks so, too—he's

*Possibly half the class!

chosen his own pillow on the bed, and he's bonded with one of the gargoyles (which, I don't think he'll mind me saying, looks very much like him).

"Let's explore," I say bravely.

"We can't," says Winnie, looking up from her neat unpacking. "We might get into trouble." Winnie does not like getting into trouble.

"*Woo-wooo-wooo!!*" Amara emerges from the inside of a HUGE wardrobe, wearing a ten-sizes-too-big cloak and flapping her arms. "I am the ghost of Principal Crawe!" she says in a silly voice and then collapses into giggles.

"I wonder where Puck and Fabi are sleeping," says Winnie after we've searched the wardrobe for more left-behind old treasures and found nothing except a cazillion cobwebs and some balls of dust as big as my head.

"Let's go and find them," I suggest.

"We really shouldn't." But I can tell she wants to.

"Just one quick expedition to say good night to them?" pleads Amara.

Winnie hesitates. "We don't know what room they're in."

"Amaaara? Winnieeeee? Beeeea?" A familiar voice floats through the window I'd just opened to drop out the dustballs. "*Can any of you hear me?*"

I look out and grin down at Puck, whose head is sticking out of a little window almost directly below.

Problem solved!

8:41 p.m.

Just got back from checking out Puck and Fabi's room.

I know it's not a competition, but we DEFINITELY WON.

Their room is much smaller than ours—it's barely *half* a hexagon—and it doesn't have a big, cozy fireplace, just a tiny little grate that they haven't even bothered to light. Also, there are little tufts of moss growing out of the gaps in the stone walls. There isn't even a real bed.... Instead, there are three *hammocks* tied to old broomsticks hovering in the middle of the room!

Fabi and Puck think that's really cool.* What they don't think is cool is that they're sharing with *Hunter*.

"It was an accident," Puck explained in a whisper. "We got distracted looking at a display of witch armor, and this was the only room left."

"I can hear you." Hunter looked up from tipping everything out of his suitcases into a heap in the middle of the room. "It's not fair. I should have a room to myself. I'm a very light sleeper." He flung himself onto his hammock and pulled on a satin eyemask.

I think Puck and Fabi are going to be very jealous when they see our room.

8:45 p.m.

Dolly's just brought us hot chocolate and what she calls "bedtime buns." For a spooky ruin in the middle of nowhere, **Cadabra** is beginning to feel pretty comfy!

PHEW!!

*But they don't have a HUGE, PILLOW-Y FOUR-POSTER BED.

"Sleep tight and don't let the ghosties bite!" she trills and turns off the lights.

8:52 p.m.

Scribbling by the light of the fire. It's getting hard to keep my eyes open, but I want to send a missive to Ash right away and let him know my new address so he can write back to me.

What *is* my new address??

9:00 p.m.

Winnie says it's:

Bea Black (visitor)
The Hexagonal Tower Room
with lots of gargoyles
Fourth Floor
West-turret-still-standing
Cadabra Castle

Okay, where to start? The bus journey or the four-poster bed?

Squeak-creak-thud.... Squeak-creak-THUD....

There's a very strange noise coming from somewhere nearby. Maybe it's a mouse?

Creak....

A really BIG one?

"Are you awake?!" I reach out and grab the witch next to me.

"I am now," says Winnie, startled. "What?"

"Listen!"

9:05 p.m.

But the strange noises have stopped. Other than the occasional hoot from a passing owl and a sleepy **ribbit** from Stan, we can't hear a thing.

"Your imagination's playing tricks on you." Winnie yawns. "Go to sleep."

10:11 p.m.

Squeak-creak-thud....

10:38 p.m.

No more spooky noises, but the flames are flickering and the gargoyles are casting weird shadows in the gloom. It's nothing like Piggoty Lane.

11 p.m.

The others are fast asleep, but although I feel like I've been awake for a HUNDRED HOURS, I'm too twitchy to settle down. Everything feels very strange.

11:08 p.m.

"Bea?" All my tossing and turning has woken up Amara. "Can you not sleep?"

There's a groan from the other mound in the bed—we've woken Winnie up, too. "What's the matter?" she asks, sitting up. "Are you missing home Bea?"

"Kind of," I mumble.

I can feel myself starting to turn red but then Amara says, "I would be homesick, too, if I wasn't sharing a room. You can borrow Percy if you like."

She pulls a tattered little teddy bear out from under her pillow and hands it to me.

"Don't worry." Winnie grins at us both. "I don't think we'll have time to miss home much." She flicks her wand, straightens all the bedcovers, and plumps my pillow. "We'll be too busy having adventures!"

I look at my friends' smiley, sleepy faces and at Stan boinging up and down happily on his special pillow like he doesn't have a care in the world.

Well.... I might still be a little homesick, but I can't help being excited and curious, too....

Let the witchy adventures begin!!

11:19 p.m.

The others have fallen back to sleep and there's just enough light from the fire to write by. Thank goodness I packed a spare diary because this one is already almost filled up, just room for one very important list.

REASONS WHY THIS IS GOING TO BE THE BEST SCHOOL TRIP EVER!

- It's an EXTRAORDINARY WITCHY trip!
- I'm with my friends (TEAM FINKELSPARK!) and Ash is taking care of Dad. I can do this.
- **Cadabra** is the CASTLIEST castle in the world with bedtime buns and four-poster beds and tons of secrets to solve but **NO GHOSTS**

Creeeeak-thuddity-squeak, squeak....

Fingers crossed!!

READ ON FOR A SNEAK PEEK AT BEA'S NEXT MAGICAL ADVENTURE!

Diary of an Accidental Witch
GHOSTLY GETAWAY

TUESDAY, JANUARY 18

8:02 a.m.

Just got woken up by a squeal from Amara so loud that Stan shot up in the air and landed on my nose.

"*Wow!*" She's pointing at one of the tapestries on the wall. The dusty flowers and creatures that we'd seen last night are gone and instead, in gold thread....

Welcome, Winnie, Amara, and Bea!
We hope you have a wonderful stay at Cadabra.
Please find below your schedule for the week!

TUESDAY

8:30 a.m.
BREAKFAST
(Buttery)

10:00 a.m.
LECTURE
Prof. Crisp. Cadabra
Through the Ages
Part One
(Library)

Midday PICNIC
(Lower Ramparts)

1 p.m. MYSTERY
CHALLENGE
Dr. Pellicano
(The Great Outdoors)

7 p.m. DINNER
Followed by QUIZ
(Banquet Hall)

WEDNESDAY

8:30 a.m.
BREAKFAST
(Buttery)

10:00 a.m.
LECTURE
Prof. Crisp. Cadabra
Through the Ages
Part Two
(Library)

Midday PICNIC
(Lower Ramparts)

1 p.m. MYSTERY
CHALLENGE
Dr. Pellicano
(Old Jousting Field)

6:30 p.m. DINNER
Followed by
LECTURE on
celestial navigation
(Banquet Hall)

THURSDAY

8:30 a.m.
BREAKFAST
(Buttery)

11:00 a.m.
MYSTERY
CHALLENGE
Ms. Sparks and
Dr. Pellicano
(The Great Outdoors)
*picnics and snacks
supplied

6:30 p.m.
CAMPFIRE
PARTY
(Secret Knoll)

FRIDAY

8:30 a.m.
BREAKFAST
(Buttery)

Midday PICNIC
(Lower Ramparts)

Followed by
CLEANING,
PACKING, and
FOND FAREWELLS

1:00 p.m. BUS
DEPARTS

"Oooooh, I love schedules," says Winnie happily.

"Ooooh, I love mystery challenges!" Amara grins.

I *think* I love mystery challenges, too, but *witchy* mystery challenges? Wait … the gold thread is weaving before our eyes….

Quick as a flash, witchlings! Out of your jammies or you'll be late for breakfast.

8:31 a.m. The Buttery

We found the buttery by following our noses. It's a big white room next to the kitchens* and it doesn't feel ruin-y at all! The stained-glass windows are only a little broken and the sun is shining through, splashing the walls with dancing golden unicorns. There's a long table with benches on either side that could seat a hundred witches, and on a little raised platform at the end of the room, there's a smaller round table surrounded by much comfier chairs. Almost hidden behind coffeepots and

*With no butter anywhere to be seen.

newspapers are the teachers and Dolly Pumpkin.

"Over here!" Puck waves. "We saved you spots."

I'd been worried that breakfast would be more witch sausages, but it looks like it's *CAKE*! A special yellow striped breakfast cake that tastes like honey that Dolly promises will give us all as much energy as baby dragons, washed down with a drink that looks like tea, but somehow tastes like toast. *Yum*.

9:35 a.m.

It's almost time for Professor Crisp's history lecture in the library. Where *is* the library?

9:55 a.m.

Found a room full of maps, a room full of brooms, and a room full of bats, but can't find the library.

"Who needs a map of the castle?" trills Dolly, flitting past.

"*Us, please!*"

10:01 a.m. The library

I've never been so excited by a library in my life.* It's at least two stories high, and its shelves are crammed with old-fashioned-looking books with titles like: *Dentistry for Dragons, How to Bond with Bavarian Bluffwaffles,* and oh! *The Friendly Finkelspark of Cadabra.* I'd have started reading then and there, but Professor Crisp was on his feet and motioning us to sit down and *hush*.

"The first time we can really begin to trace the history of **Cadabra Castle**," he begins in his low, slow voice, "is during the foreign occupation of the country. *Castrum Cadabrorum* was one of the greatest forts built—renowned even in its day for its excellent working toilets." He flicks his wand, and one wall of shelves disappears to be replaced by a whiteboard.

*And I really like libraries!

Timeline of Cadabra Castle

43-44 AD—Cadabra Castle is established as a fort.

410 AD—Invaders withdraw from the country and the fort falls into disrepair.

490-520 AD—The High Witch Merlin uses the ruins as a stopping-off point on his journeys and as a retreat to replenish his magical energies.

898 AD—The fort is rebuilt as a castle by the witch warrior Aethlric the Angry. **Bad things happen.**

"I think it's best if we skip over much of what happened at **Cadabra** during the reign of Aethlric the Angry," says the professor. "We'll come back to this difficult and rather dark period in ninth grade. All you need to know now is that, even by the standards of very angry witch warriors, Aethlric was the MOST FURIOUS of all. Not the kind of witch you'd want to meet on the battlefield."

"Tell us more!" we chorus.

"You really are a REVOLTINGLY BLOODTHIRSTY class! No, no, we need to move on because you'll never understand **Cadabra** without knowing that it's the first-and-forever home of *witchy cooperation—*" He breaks off to tell Hunter to stop wand-sword-fighting with his neighbor. "Where was I? Ah, yes, *cooperation and communication—*and never were those virtues more needed in the witch world than in the aftermath of Aethlric's rule."

He flicks his wand, and a new entry appears on the timeline:

> 898-1523 AD—A period marred by strife. The witch community is broken into a number of tribes that practice different kinds of magic, including: water-witchery, fire-witchery, sword-witchery, herb-witchery, dance-witchery, animal-witchery, cake-witchery, etc. These tribes do NOT get along and are constantly fighting for power.

"*Dance-witchery!*" Amara jumps up and does a little twirl. "I choose that one."

"I pick SWORD-WITCHERY!" yells Hunter.

"*Cake-witchery!*" shouts Puck. "I've found my tribe!"

"The whole point," says the professor with a sigh, "is that it is NOT A GOOD THING for witches to divide themselves into tribes. Witches should learn from each other and *share* their skills, and it was at **Cadabra** that the first steps were taken toward this when the tribal leaders agreed that they were all spending too much time and energy and dragons' gold fighting one another and that they'd be stronger—and better able to survive in a world where they were not always well understood—if they put their pointy hats together. Look and learn...."

Another flick of his wand, and the timeline grows longer....

> 1531 AD—Representatives of all the witch tribes gather at Cadabra for peace negotiations. Over a legendary feast in the banquet hall, they demonstrate their arts to one another and realize how much greater their powers could be if they shared their knowledge and worked together.
>
> The scroll recording the Great Peace Treaty of 1531, setting out the rules of witchy cooperation and establishing the Law of All Witches, is still held in the Cadabra Castle library today.

"So ... it's the LAW that we have to be friends with each other?" Winnie makes a careful note.

"*WHAAAAT!*" Hunter sounds shocked.

"*All of us?!*" (I swear Blair looked at me when she said that.)

"*All the time?*" We're all worried now!

Professor Crisp looks at our faces and laughs.

ABOUT THE AUTHOR*

Bea Black is eleven years old and has recently moved to Little Spellshire, where she lives with her dad, a weather scientist. She has no pets, but has a very special relationship with the class frog. Her lifelong dream is to get a puppy. This is Bea's fifth diary.

*With a little help from Perdita and Honor Cargill!